To Daisy

From.......................

It was Christmas Eve and Daisy
was snug and warm in her cosy bed.
She was trying so hard to go to sleep,
but she could hear strange noises.

It wasn't the sound of sleigh bells.
It wasn't the sound of reindeer hoofs on the roof.
It wasn't even the sound of Santa unpacking his sack.

It was more of a

HARRUMPH!

and an

OOF!

It was no use.

There would be no sleep for Daisy
until she had found out what
was making that noise.

Daisy crept down the stairs
and peered into the living room.
There were three stockings
hanging from the fireplace.

One of them belonged to Daisy. But where had the other two come from? Suddenly, a muffled voice came from the chimney.

Daisy

"Oh, dear. I'm even **more** stuck now!"

There was a scuffling sound from behind the Christmas tree, and Daisy jumped when a small elf appeared.

Daisy

"Uh, hello," said the elf. "I guess you've caught us!"

Daisy listened as the elf explained
that Santa was stuck in the chimney.
The elf had tried to pull him out, but the
only things that had come down so far
were Santa's boots and trousers!

"I can help you," suggested Daisy.
"I'll hold Santa's feet and we can both pull."
The elf agreed. "Between us we might
be able to get him unstuck."

Daisy firmly grasped both of Santa's feet.
Suddenly a light went on upstairs.
"Daisy, is that you?" called her mum.
"Back to bed now, please, or Santa won't come!"

Daisy

At that moment
Santa shot back up
the chimney… with
Daisy still hanging
onto his feet!

The poor elf could not believe his eyes.
But there was no time to think…
Daisy's mum was coming
out of her bedroom.

"I'm coming!" squeaked the elf. He hurried
up the stairs and jumped into Daisy's bed,
pulling the covers over his head.
"Night night, sweetie," said Daisy's mum.

Meanwhile, up on the roof, Santa and Daisy
had landed in a heap. The clever reindeer had
hooked their reins under Santa's arms and
pulled as hard as they could.

"Good work!" said Santa, brushing
himself off. "No more mince pies
for me tonight!"

Daisy scrambled to her feet, but Santa
was so busy that he didn't notice Daisy
and the elf had switched places!

"I think we had better deliver the rest
of the presents first," said Santa,
"and leave this house for last."

Santa climbed into the driver's seat.

"Elf, you get the presents ready for our next destination," he called over his shoulder.

"But I'm not Elf..." replied Daisy.

Santa wasn't listening.
He was talking to the reindeer.
"Up, up and away!" Santa called,
and the reindeer took off before
Daisy had time to explain.

Daisy held on tight as the
sleigh soared high over the rooftops
and into the night sky.

Surrounded by sacks, Daisy was
so busy working out which presents were
which that there was no time to let Santa
know a mistake had been made.

There were big
presents for the cities,

and **SHINY** presents
for the towns.

There were **ODD**-shaped
presents for the villages,

and **unusual**
presents for the farms.

To
Daisy

As they landed at their next stop, Santa decided that he couldn't risk getting stuck in a chimney again.

"Elf, I think you had better make the deliveries from now on," Santa said. "I'll sort the presents."

Daisy *shimmied* down chimneys.

She **squeezed** through cat flaps.

And, if all else failed, she used Santa's *magic* key to let herself in.

In each house Daisy picked up the mince pies to take to Mrs Claus and carrots for the reindeer.

Finally there was just one sack left, and
Santa still hadn't realised his mistake!
The sleigh headed back over the
rooftops to Daisy's house.

Sliding down her chimney with
a sack of her own presents was
the most fun Daisy had ever had.

She put her presents under
the Christmas tree, then picked
up Santa's trousers and boots
and placed them in the sack.

Daisy

To
Daisy

"Psst! Elf, where are you?" whispered Daisy.

A very happy Elf appeared, rubbing his eyes. "I've had such a nice nap," he said. Daisy handed over the sack and waved as Elf disappeared up the chimney.

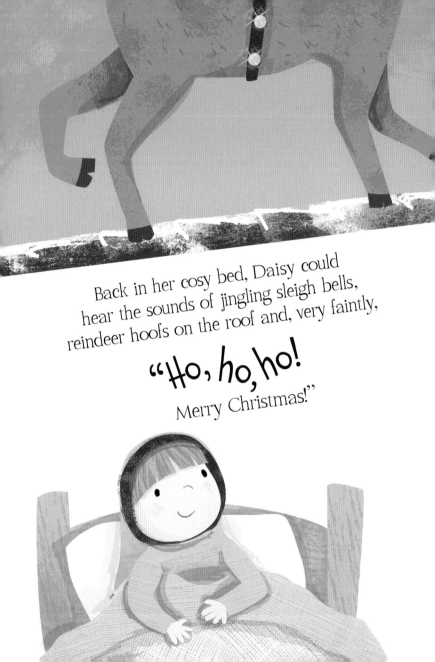

Back in her cosy bed, Daisy could
hear the sounds of jingling sleigh bells,
reindeer hoofs on the roof and, very faintly,

"Ho, ho, ho!
Merry Christmas!"

Or was that,

"Ho, ho, ho!
Yummy mince pies!"?

Write your name on the labels.

Draw yourself as an elf.

Written by Katherine Sully
Illustrated by Julia Seal
Designed by Nicola Moore

This edition published by HOMETOWN WORLD in 2018
Hometown World Ltd
1 Queen Street
Bath
BA1 1HE

www.hometownworld.co.uk

Follow us @hometownworldbooks

ISBN 978-1-78553-597-0
All rights reserved
Printed in Italy
HTW_PO201814

put me
in the story
Bestselling books starring your child!